MARTIN WADDELL

Illustrated by Scoular Anderson

OXFORD
UNIVERSITY PRESS

Great Clarendon Street, Oxford OX2 6DP

Oxford University Press is a department of the University of Oxford.
It furthers the University's objective of excellence in research, scholarship,
and education by publishing worldwide in

Oxford New York
Auckland Cape Town Dar es Salaam Hong Kong Karachi
Kuala Lumpur Madrid Melbourne Mexico City Nairobi
New Delhi Shanghai Taipei Toronto

With offices in
Argentina Austria Brazil Chile Czech Republic France Greece
Guatemala Hungary Italy Japan Poland Portugal Singapore
South Korea Switzerland Thailand Turkey Ukraine Vietnam



British Library Cataloguing in Publication Data
Data available

ISBN 978-0-19-911346-0

9 10 8

Available in packs
Stage 10 More Stories B Pack of 6:
ISBN 978-0-19-911343-9
Stage 10 More Stories B Class Pack:
ISBN 978-0-19-911344-6
Guided Reading Cards also available:
ISBN 978-0-19-911352-1

Printed in China by Imago

Paper used in the production of this book is a natural,
recyclable product made from wood grown in sustainable forests.
The manufacturing process conforms to the environmental
regulations of the country of origin.

# 1

# The ghost ship

One day Ernie was late for school. He ran up School Hill and slipped through the hole in the fence. He hoped the Head wouldn't see him.

'Wow!' Ernie gasped.

There was a ghost ship floating about in the playground. It was much like an ordinary ship, but white and see-through. He knew that it couldn't be real.

The ghost ship was tied to one of the netball posts. A strange glow came from it, and it rocked up and down as if it was riding invisible waves. A ghost seagull flew around it.

'Ahoy there, ghost ship!' Ernie cried bravely.

A ghost's head popped out from a window. 'Who said that?' the ghost asked.

'I did!' said Ernie.

'But you're not supposed to be able to see me!' the ghost gasped.

Then the ghost thought again.

'Are you *sure* you can see me?' the ghost asked.

'Quite sure,' Ernie said.

The window slammed shut.

'I spoke to a ghost!' Ernie shouted.

Mrs Wiggins, the caretaker, heard Ernie shout. She came running out to the playground.

'I sp-sp-spoke to a ghost!' Ernie stuttered.

'Shhh! Don't tell anyone,' said Mrs Wiggins.

'Why not?' Ernie asked.

'I don't want you upsetting the small ones in Class One!' Mrs Wiggins said.

'But the ghost ship's parked in the playground,' Ernie said. 'They'll *see* it when they come out at break.'

'Not everyone can see it,' said Mrs Wiggins.

'Well, I *can*,' Ernie told her.

'Then that makes two of us,' sighed Mrs Wiggins.

Mrs Wiggins marched up to the ghost ship.

'Ship ahoy!' called Mrs Wiggins.

The window popped open, and out looked the same ghost as before.

'Ahoy, there, Mrs Wiggins,' the ghost said, politely.

'Captain Pegleg!' Mrs Wiggins scolded. 'You promised that no one else but me could see you. But one of the children from Class Four just has! Haven't you, Ernie?'

'Yes,' Ernie said, 'I just have.'

'Well, it *can* happen, you know,' the Captain said, sounding upset. 'Not often, but sometimes it happens.'

'You can't keep sailing in here if people can see you!' Mrs Wiggins said, firmly.

'I can't *help* sailing in here,' the Captain told her.

'Why not?' Ernie asked.

'There's just me on board!' said the Captain. 'I can't sail her alone, so I have to go where she blows. I just wish she'd blow in here more often. Then I could hunt for my treasure.'

The Captain went on, 'I'm doomed to sail the seas forever until I find my lost treasure. I know it's here because that's what it says on my map.'

'You'd better find it this time, or else!' warned Mrs Wiggins.

The window snapped shut.

'Ghost treasure!' said Ernie. 'Wait till I tell this to Class Four!'

# 2

# 'We can't see it!'

Everyone had to wait until break time to see the ghost ship. They rushed out of class and into the playground.

'There it is!' Ernie shouted, pointing at the ghost ship.

Everyone took a good look. They saw the bins and the fence, but they couldn't see any ship.

‘*We* can’t see it,’ said Louie.

‘But there IS a ghost ship!’ Ernie said, looking at it, and *through* it, both at the same time. The ghost ship was see-through and fuzzy.

‘There’s no ghost ship here!’ said Louie.

The ghost seagull flew down and landed on Louie’s head.

'A ghost seagull just landed on your head!' Ernie told Louie.

'Oh no it didn't!' said Louie, who couldn't see it, or feel it.

'OH YES IT DID!' Ernie shouted.

'OH NO IT DIDN'T!' roared everyone else.

They laughed at Ernie for making up stories about ghost seagulls and ships. Then they ran off to play.

Along came Jade, the smallest and cleverest girl in Class Four. 'What's that ghost ship doing here?' she asked Ernie.

'You can see it too!' Ernie gasped.

'Of course I can,' said Jade.

'No one else can, but me and Mrs Wiggins,' Ernie said. 'It's Captain Pegleg's ship and he's doomed to sail the sea forever, until he finds his lost treasure. He thinks he left it around here.'

'We could help him to find it,' said little Jade.

'How?' Ernie asked.

'My dad has books about treasure hunting,' said Jade. 'We'll look in his books and find out what to do.'

'Ghost treasure hunt starts right now!' shouted Ernie.

'Ghost treasure hunt starts when we've looked at Dad's books!' said Jade.

The bell went for the start of lessons.

'After school!' Jade told him. 'After school, and no mucking about!'

# 3

# The treasure hunt

After school, they went to Jade's house and got out her dad's books about treasure hunting.

'That's how we'll do it!' said Jade, showing Ernie a page in one of the books.

'But we haven't got one of those,' Ernie said, pointing at the metal detector.

'My dad has,' Jade said. 'He uses it when he hunts for old coins and things on the beach. That's why he has all these books about treasure hunting.'

They ran back up School Hill to the school. Ernie was carrying a spade and Jade had a big bag, with the metal detector in it.

'Captain Pegleg!' Ernie called.

The Captain was on deck. 'You again!' said Captain Pegleg. 'Can you still see me?'

'Yes,' Ernie said.

'We know you can't stop sailing till you find your ghost treasure,' Jade told the Captain.

'We want to help you find it,' Ernie added.

'But first we want to look at your map,' said Jade.

The map was ripped and torn, with lots of holes in it.

'The ghost seagull got at it!' Captain Pegleg said.

'It says: *X Marks the treasure* on the map,' said Jade, 'but I don't see any X.'

'The ghost seagull pecked out my X. I can't remember where it was,' sighed Captain Pegleg. 'I can't even find Treasure Island … But I'm sure this is where it used to be.'

'It is!' said little Jade, and she grinned. 'Treasure Island is here, where we're standing!'

'How do you know?' asked Ernie.

'Look!' Jade said, and she drew on the back of the Captain's map.

'The bit sticking up is School Hill!' she told Ernie. 'Where our houses are now, used to be under the sea, years ago. My dad told me.'

'We still don't know where to look!' Ernie said. 'We could dig all day and never find the treasure.'

'We'll use my dad's metal detector,' explained Jade. 'It'll go *ping* when we're near the treasure.'

'*If* metal detectors work on ghost gold!' muttered Ernie.

'Well, it *might* work,' said Jade. 'At least we can try.'

So they looked for the treasure ...

But they didn't find it ... so they looked again ... and again ...

... They looked again ... and again ...

Then *PING PING PING* went the metal detector.

It was the treasure!

They dug up Captain Pegleg's ghost treasure chest filled with gold. It was ghost gold, so it wasn't as heavy as real gold. They started to carry it back to the ship.

At least, that's what they started to do. But as they were walking back towards the school, the ghost treasure chest began fading away. Captain Pegleg began fading, too.

'Goodbye, Captain Pegleg,' Jade whispered.

'The ghost ship faded away because we found Captain Pegleg's treasure,' Ernie told Class Four the next day.

'There never *was* a ghost ship,' said Louie.

'Oh yes, there WAS!' shouted Ernie.

'Oh no, there WASN'T!' shouted everyone else.

Somewhere else, somewhere far away, a ghost seagull cried. But nobody heard it, except Ernie and Jade and Mrs Wiggins.

## *About the author*

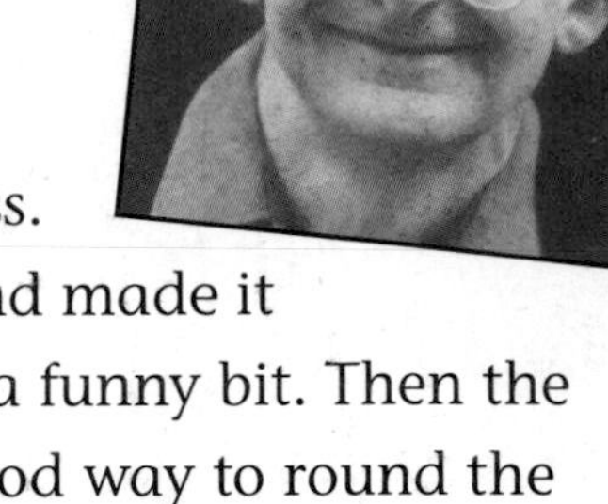

I plan a lot before writing, but usually the best bits surprise me as I write.

In this one, the ghost seagull flew in as a jokey way of explaining why the Captain's map was useless. After that, I went back and made it land on Louie's head, as a funny bit. Then the seagull's cry seemed a good way to round the story off.

So, the seagull that wasn't in my plan at all, became the bit that makes the story work.